Touching Places
foreign and familiar

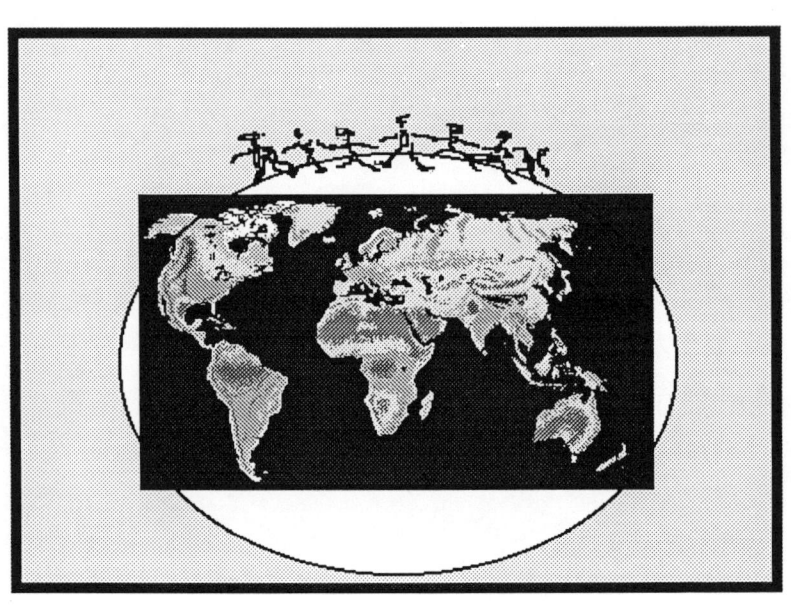

Touching Places
foreign and familiar

vignettes by
JOAN KRIEGER

Fithian Press • Santa Barbara, 1993

Copyright © 1993 Joan Krieger
All Rights Reserved
Printed in the United States of America

Book design and typography by Eric Larson

Published by Fithian Press
Post Office Box 1525
Santa Barbara, CA 93102

LIBRARY OF CONGRESS CATALOGING-IN-PUBLICATION DATA
  Krieger, Joan.
    Touching places foreign and familiar : vignettes / Joan Krieger.
      p. cm.
    ISBN 1-56474-066-8
    1. Travel—Fiction. I. Title
  PS3561.R5534T68 1993
  831'.54—dc20   93-13418
                                        CIP

*To Murray,
whose trace can be found
in my every footstep
through almost fifty years
of venturing through life
together.*

Contents

Preface   9
The Mandolin Hangs on the Wall   13
Ohio! Yes, It Is!   23
Definitely Not Kabuki   33
Topkapi and Me   41
India—Side by Side   51
The Refrigerator—*"Silence Absolu"*   59
Encore Paris   69
Germany—*"Natürlich"*   77
Mr. Ho and the PRC   85

Preface

It has now been over forty years since I underwent the first of many encounters with members of what were to me then alien cultures: persons with whom I sought, and often found, lasting friendship. My wish then, as it has been since, was to domesticate myself to their ways, although too often, I later came to see, I was actually trying to domesticate them to mine. This realization has increasingly made me aware of the special delicacy in those human relationships that accompany these meetings of cultural differences that are searching for unity.

In the pages that follow I have tried to explore that delicacy. In them I have collected a number of what seem to me luminous moments—from past decades as well as from recent years—in which the traveler/writer collides or curiously meshes with the strangeness that greets and sometimes taunts her. These occur in places that I have touched and that are still touching to me—the more exotic, Hyderbad, Guangzhou, Istanbul and Ankara, Tokyo, Moscow; and the more familiar, Paris, Konstanz, and even Columbus, Ohio.

Are these a record of incidents in my past? To a considerable extent, yes. But there are also many things altered in them, not for purposes of wish-fulfillment, I believe, but to help make a better story than history might have allowed. I invented what was needed to give them a form that would reveal more amply the paradoxical human interaction I was trying to get at. I would say, then, that they lie in some no-man's land between memoir and fiction.

I send them forth with the hope that these happenings, at times whimsical, at times serious, may captivate others as they have captivated me.

I want to record my thanks to my husband, Murray, and my daughter, Catherine, who shared some of these experiences with me. I am also deeply grateful to Jim Barnes, who as editor of *The Chariton Review* published the first vignette in this volume, "The Mandolin Hangs on the Wall" (in Vol. 18, No. 2, Fall 1992), and has given his permission for it to be reprinted here. He accepted it with so warmly positive a response that I was encouraged to work on the others in order to produce this book.

Laguna Beach, California
October 1, 1993

Touching Places
foreign and familiar

The Mandolin Hangs on the Wall

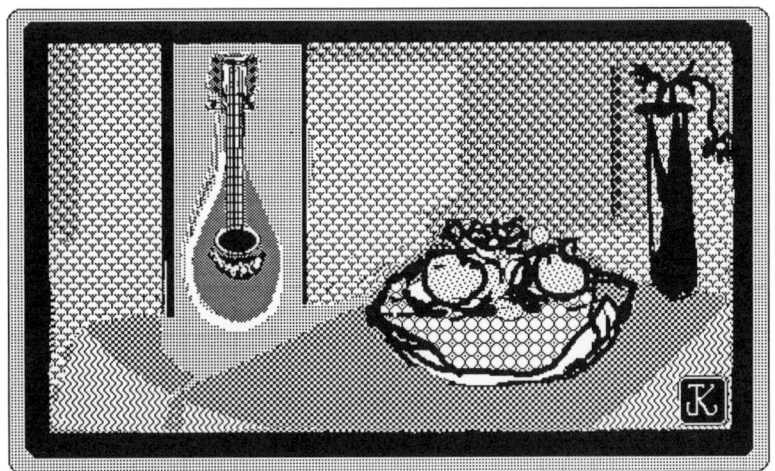

The Mandolin Hangs on the Wall

If, long before I was born, my father hadn't missed the sailing and sinking of the *Titanic* in 1912, I would not exist, of course, and neither would these echoes of the past. When he did come it was with no baggage; just a few remnants of another world. Recalling them now compels me to put into writing some moments of my youth that have followed me into my very mature years and still haunt me.

My father, Artur Stampf, was born in Berlin to the son of a German playwright and the daughter of a Polish scholar. Unfortunately his father died (and was buried with some ceremony in Leipzig) when my father was only seven years of age. He was thereafter brought up in Poland by his mother who, despite many marriage proposals, chose to remain a widow. He grew up in Warsaw but returned to Germany to attend the University of Heidelberg, which was his father's alma mater.

Upon returning to Poland my father was conscripted into the Russian army. In contrast to the darker looks of his parents, my father had a shock of blond hair and ice blue eyes. Because of his handsome demeanor, as well as his facility in several languages and his mastery of the cornet and mandolin, he was selected for the tsar's orchestra in Tsarskoye Selo, the summer palace outside of St. Petersburg (later renamed Leningrad and recently renamed St. Petersburg again). His service there lasted six months. But when the captain asked my father to become interested in his daughter, my father, having refused, had visions of a future in Siberia. So he had his mother ask friends of his late father to make arrangements for him to meet her in Paris. He stole an officer's uniform and, with little misadventure, deserted the army.

His mother met him in Paris, and they went on to London. Because he contracted the flu, he missed the sailing of the *Titanic* and arrived on the next boat at their destination, New York City. My father carried only a few precious reminders of his days in the tsar's service: two purple velvet volumes of Russian folk tales with gold tassels and gold-tipped pages, which had belonged to Tsar Nikolai II and had been given to him by the captain of the orchestra, and a dark gray cloth case bound in tan leather that contained a mandolin.

My father became involved in some theater work, and for many years thereafter in the production of radio programs. He told me that he met my mother in Brooklyn on the night of a great blizzard, when he mistakenly went to the wrong house. She was playing the piano, and he, carrying his mandolin for an evening with old friends, was asked into the warmth and did not leave until late in the night.

In 1929, when I was three, my mother died of what was thought to be a ruptured appendix, and my grandmother came to live with us and brought me up. My grandmother spoke Polish and German and French to my father when they did not want me to understand their conversation. In reaction I learned languages quickly. In school I read German and studied French, and because my mother had been a teacher, I was determined to become one as well.

But the romance, mystery, and exoticism in my life came from those two volumes whose pages I so often pored over with their joyful drawings and a script that was unintelligible; and, yes, from the dark gray case that was always very carefully placed in the corner of our front closet.

My father never quite understood how an "American girl" should be educated, or what to do about it. From the time I was seven years old, at bedtime he told me the stories of the operas. At eleven he told me, "Don't read *The Bobbsey Twins at the County Fair*. Read Pushkin; read Tolstoy." But what he didn't know was that, as far back as I can remember, when I was sent to bed I would hear his friends through my open door, friends he knew from a restaurant they frequented, The Russian Korchma, on 14th Street. After having had dinner and speaking mainly in Russian, one of them would say, "Artur, the mandolin." And out would come the exquisitely polished melon-shaped mahogany instrument and a pear-shaped, tortoise-shell pick. And he played and they sang for hours.

This happened, I remember, quite frequently during my early years. When I was in my teens I remember being invited to the house of a lady named Manya, who showed me photos and spoke of her childhood in St. Petersburg, avoiding the Soviet name, Leningrad. She had a samovar, and I drank tea from a tall glass seated in a gleaming brass cuff, and she sang and my father played songs of love, of joy, of sorrow, of chrysanthemums, of the birch trees, and the swishing of the horse-drawn sleigh with the *troika* bells gently jingling in the softly falling snow.

In the depression years of the thirties, the occasions became fewer and fewer, but my enchantment became more intense. In the years through elementary school and high school I did read the works of Pushkin and Tolstoy—and Dostoevsky and Turgenev as well. I attended performances by the Ballet Russe de Monte Carlo, and was immersed in the aura of that "Russian World" every time we had dinner in The Russian Tearoom, a well-known restaurant on 57th Street where artists, writers, and tourists met. But through those years there were many evenings when I coaxed my father to play the mandolin and translate all the songs and talk about *that* time—by which, of course, I meant the time of the tsar.

The last time I saw Manya was in the winter of 1941 after the signing of the Russo-German pact. She arrived, as so often before, older, of course, but still a commanding figure with flashing black eyes, very black hair severely pulled back from her face (hair that I assumed was, as we then said, "touched up"), and a strong, exotic perfume. She embraced me, saying, in her very potently accented English, "Yanushka! How you have grown!" As I had done so many times before, I hung her coat in the closet and placed her drum-shaped *karakul* fur hat and matching warm, luxurious muff on the entry table in the hall. The muff (an accessory so out of fashion that it can certainly be called archaic today) was never put down before I placed both my hands inside and softly rubbed it against my cheek.

The war was on, and we had recently moved to be closer to the Navy yard where my father worked for the war effort. We had a rather somber meal as he and Manya talked about Europe and I talked about not being old enough to join the Waves (the women's unit of the Navy).

With the crystal clink of the after-dinner cognac glasses and a whispered *nazdorovye,* Manya asked my father, "Perhaps a song or two?" That was my cue, and I very quickly pranced to the closet and brought out the case. To my horror I pulled out what looked like a dead swan. It had a broken neck and two large mahogany strips hung from the belly like two black wings. It had to have been damaged in the move.

I asked, "Can it be repaired, Dad?" He replied in a rather curious tone, "No, my dear. It has suffered the ravages of war."

In the fifties and sixties I finished my university courses, became a teacher, married a teacher, had children, and moved into my later years. The cold war was on, and there seemed to be little time to think of more than the here and now. There were, however, other intrusions I did not escape. Once in Paris in 1958 I accidentally strayed into the Russian quarter and walked into the Greek Orthodox Church on Rue Daru. I sat quietly in a pew of this almost-empty golden-domed edifice, then crossed the street to a small corner restaurant, where I spotted two ballet students chatting in French and ordering in Russian. I ate blini, borscht, and black bread, and drank a glass of black tea, and deeply inhaled the Russianness of the place. I told no one of the afternoon, and returned to my life.

In the seventies I remember avoiding reading Solzhenitzyn for reasons I didn't want to understand. But in 1972 my husband and children, now quite grown, decided during a family outing that we ought to see the film of Pasternak's novel, *Doctor Zhivago.* We did. And no one, including me, could comprehend why I, generally considered a well-balanced individual, should have exploded into an uncontrollable convulsion of tears.

In 1990 my husband was asked to deliver a paper at the Gorki Institute in Moscow. Of course I was thrilled to go along for my first trip to Russia—thrilled and, despite all I had heard and knew, full of expectations. After we arrived at that grim city, we endured a succession of the "best" restaurants—hushed, slovenly places that served none of the expected dishes and provided no music; unkempt museums, whose extravagant displays I could relate in no way to the quietly desperate life outside its walls; and, above all, people with set faces who looked as if they neither sang nor danced.

We were escorted by a young woman, a student at the university. She had the stance and walk of a person who had studied ballet, though she was studying archeology. She had platinum blond hair pulled severely into a braid at the back of her head. Her eyes were clear aquamarine, and her name could have been Lara, Zhivago's Lara. But it was Sonia. She wore the same dress and turned-out shoes whenever we met. She spoke little, though her English was rather good. She smiled less. She read only what was important to her work. But when I asked if she liked music, her eyes lit up and sparkled. I asked, "Do you play an instrument?" Sonia replied, "Oh! Yes...well, not exactly. I have a mandolin." I asked, almost inaudibly, feeling I couldn't take another breath until she replied, "Tell me, Sonia, do you play it?" She answered very brightly, with a small smile. "The mandolin belonged to my grandfather and my mother gave it to me; and it always hangs on the wall."

Today, many months after my return from Russia, I find myself in what was my father's house, the home of the broken mandolin. Here I let my mind go back to Moscow and to that other mandolin, still intact but long out of use, so that it could add nothing to anyone else's memory, though it had disrupted mine. I think back to my leaving Moscow soon after my conversation with Sonia, who I now know was not at all Lara. And I also know why, after such alienating moments and violated memories, Russia was too much for me. I had to flee. So, despite a most gracious invitation to visit, I dared not see St. Petersburg, old neighbor to Tsarskoye Selo and Manya's beloved home, now renamed again the way she would have liked it to be. I could not bring myself to go. And I suspect I never will. I will just keep remembering the enchantment and the loss.

Ohio! Yes, It Is!

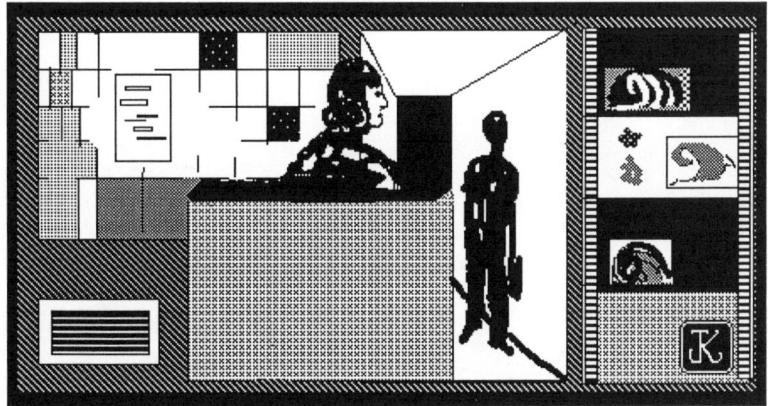

Ohio! Yes, It Is!

Yesterday, when I was doing some early Christmas shopping, I paused momentarily at the bookshop window of my local mall. I had to hurry on for an appointment, and I did not have the time to go inside. But, try as I did, with so many other things to do, I could not stop thinking about the beautifully bound two-volume set of books that was displayed in the window. In large letters across the book jacket was written *"The Economic History of Japan Since WWII* by A. Yakamoto." Now, why should that have arrested my attention, I kept asking myself? The subject held no particular interest for me. But the name, Yakamoto, kept echoing in my head: "A. Yakamoto." And suddenly this morning, after almost forty years, it all began to come back.

In the early 1950s I was a graduate student in fine arts at Ohio State University in Columbus, Ohio. To help get me through school I had gotten a part-time job in the library as an assistant to the curator of prints in the rare-book section. I was at a desk in front of the rare-book room, and next to my desk against the wall was a large glass display case for which I was responsible. Once a month I chose a subject from the available collections, selected appropriate prints, and set up the exhibit in the case. I was also assigned the minor task of collecting and distributing the mail for a seminar that met three times a week in a room down the hall from my desk.

The seminar, I soon discovered, was made up of a very select group of Japanese graduate students in economics from Kyoto University. This created a rather unusual situation, I observed, for a number of reasons. First, never before had I or anyone else I knew seen a contemporary of ours who had come from a country we had been taught to think of as our detested enemy in the Second World War, only a very few years before. This discomfort was made even more evident when the group, going to and coming from their classroom, would pass students and even faculty in the corridor, and a sudden hush would prevail.

Secondly, the difficulty of their presence was compounded by the fact that there were very few, if any, Japanese people in Columbus so soon after the war. Indeed, I do recall worrying about whether any of these Japanese students had ever seen the local telephone book, which, on its opening information page, spoke of the city of Columbus priding itself in the fact that its inhabitants were "97% native-born." "Native" at that time did not refer to the American Indian but was reserved for any "non-immigrant." I, who had been born and brought-up in the polyglot of New York City, spotted that worrisome inset with some concern the very first time I looked up a telephone number after my arrival in Columbus. It wasn't a great comfort to any cosmopolitan visitor to the city. How would visitors from so alien a land as Japan respond to these words, I remember thinking? (I'm sure this passage has long since been eliminated and forgotten.)

The mail usually arrived in the late morning while I was at work at my desk. Instead of my delivering the mail, it was picked up three times a week promptly at 2:00 P.M. by a lean, dark-eyed, black-haired, smiling young man in his twenties. With my expectations shaped by the frightening caricatures of Japanese men created by the propaganda films to which Americans were subjected during the war, I was happily surprised that I would have to describe him as handsome, and certainly less than toothy. He was very neatly dressed, and I particularly noticed that, contrary to my expectations, he was tall and did not wear eyeglasses.

For several days he brushed by my desk, picked up the mail, looked in my direction, stopped for a moment, smiled broadly, and said what sounded to me like "Ohio!" I immediately responded with "Yes, it is!" And he walked on. By the end of the second week this little scene had repeated itself several times: "Ohio!" "Yes, it is!"

At the beginning of the third week he walked by and, with what seemed to be a small wave of the hand, smiled, nodded his head, and, looking in my direction, brightly said, "Yes, it is!" and began to walk on. But my furrowed brow, dropped jaw, and very weakly questioning "Ohio?" made him stop and come back to the desk.

"Yes, it is?" he even more weakly questioned back. "Doesn't 'Yes, it is' mean 'Hello'?" he asked.

I explained that I had assumed, for some reason beyond me, that he had been referring to the state of Ohio when he greeted me. Now it was his turn to be surprised: "Oh, you must excuse my ignorance," he responded in a clear but accented English. He went on to say that he thought "Yes, it is" was a local or perhaps colloquial expression, the equivalent of "Ohio," which in Japanese is a form of greeting like "hello" or "good day." I then apologized for *my* ignorance and thanked him for introducing me to a new expression, which, incidentally, I have used from then on to greet my many Japanese friends over the years.

In the display case for that month I had put on exhibit a series of prints of the widely recognized "Wave" done by the great Japanese artist Hokusai, whose work I had studied. On that very afternoon he came by, picked up the mail, and paused at the case. He smiled and said rather excitedly, "Hokusai!"

I quickly responded with, "Yes, it is!"

"Oh no!" said he, "Hokusai." And we both began to laugh quite loudly. He added, "I am sorry to have confused you again, but I must admit that I was quite surprised at seeing the work of Hokusai in such an unexpected place." I, too, embarrassed by my automatic response, made my apologies. He introduced himself as Akira Yakamoto and came quite late to his class that day, as we quickly got lost in a discussion of the beauty, delicacy, and artistry of the work of Hokusai. And there a friendship began.

Three times a week, about ten minutes before his class, Akira stopped at my desk to chat. On many occasions he also stopped by after class, after my desk was closed for the day, and we would continue conversations started earlier which just couldn't seem to wait for the next day to be continued.

I tried to answer his many curious questions, as he did mine. He wondered why people stared at him on the bus, why they asked such absurd questions as whether he wore Western clothes in Japan, whether he knew what an escalator was, whether it ever snowed in the land of cherry blossoms? He himself wanted to know whether he should look people in the eyes when speaking to them, as they did when speaking to him. This custom was considered impolite in Japan. I explained that Japan had been closed to the West for a long time, and that we were still a young country with much to learn.

His response to that explanation was to place on my desk a copy of *Life* magazine all in Japanese, accompanied by a note saying that the publication was delivered weekly in Tokyo. Of course, I could make no sense at all of the text, but the photographs were enlightening and educating, stunning pictures of everyday life in Japan. He had his own questions about our cultural habits: why were Americans so anxious to eat sandwiches, and why were they always made on white bread (which we then referred to as "Wonder Bread")? He remarked that a slice looked and tasted so much like a paper napkin that he could not understand how anyone would eat it. I was at a loss to respond, I must admit.

His next query was just as puzzling to me. He had noticed that in our high-rise buildings the floor numbers jumped from number twelve to fourteen. Assuming that the number thirteen must have been skipped because it was considered unlucky, he asked what reason lay behind the superstition. Was it, he wondered, like the number four in Japanese, the symbol for which was the same as the word "death," so that it was avoided wherever possible? Of course, since our written language hardly allows such coincidences of meaning, there must have been some other less obvious reason that I was not aware of. Many of his questions during our more serious discussions of art and education I could answer, so that we could talk long and often. Strangely, it was these small and odd inquiries that seemed more urgent as they frequently interposed themselves.

For my part I turned to more immediately personal

matters. To begin with, I asked if he was married. He was, and he explained that his wife did not speak English and had not accompanied him, though she had been invited. She was afraid she would be lonely in Columbus, and I suspect she was correct. When I asked about what he liked in Western food, he replied that he was addicted to hamburgers. He did not like the round ones that were thick like McDonald's, but the ones made by a company called White Castle that had outlets all over the Midwest and produced a smaller, thinner, square-ish hamburger, the patty of which was smothered in sauteed onions. He said that although the bakeries had fantastic looking cakes, he could not bring himself to enjoy them.

"Not even chocolate?" I inquired, as most people I knew could be considered chocoholics.

"No," he replied, almost longingly, "the Japanese diet has for so long been lacking in sugar, it is very hard to get used to." He wondered on his part why we put sugar in our tea, when in itself it is so full of flavor. I could only answer, "Perhaps *your* tea is." I went on to concede that ours is too weak and needs enhancement. Much information, great and small, seemingly important and trivial, went back and forth during those three months of the seminar.

On the next to the last day of the seminar we decided it would be appropriate to have a farewell luncheon together. He presented me with a lovely print of a nineteenth-century temple god, which still hangs on my wall, and I gave him a drawing he had admired that I had made of the rolling Ohio countryside in the spring.

Of the many subjects we had so vigorously covered over the weeks, the one we never mentioned was the war. And on this final meeting I could no longer resist. My husband had spent most of the war in India, some of it during that failed Japanese "march on Delhi." He had worked with the people who had been instrumental in breaking the Japanese code, leading to a major naval victory that many considered to be a turning point. So I had to venture something before we parted. I asked about what he had been doing over those years. Akira looked at me and did not smile as he said haltingly, "I was trained as a Kamikaze pilot, but I never flew." After he left we did not communicate, and the days, the months, and the years have fallen away without any contact whatsoever. Until yesterday, that is. I'll continue to wonder if the author A. Yakomoto is indeed the Akira Yakomoto I now remember. And I know I will not try to find out, perhaps because I want to enjoy thinking that a fulfilled writer and scholar is what has become of that unfulfilled suicide pilot.

Definitely Not Kabuki

Definitely Not Kabuki

When in 1991 my husband and I were asked to lecture in Tokyo, we eagerly accepted. All our interchanges were to be in English. Although we spoke several languages, we were totally ignorant of Japanese. Our very gracious hosts settled us in an establishment called The International House, a hotel for invited foreign guests. It was a refurbished old estate, set surprisingly in the midst of the crowded city, with simple Western-style rooms and a giant wall surrounding a quiet, green, typical (I was told) Japanese garden.

This estate was in what is called the Roppongi section of Tokyo. During the day we were driven from place to place in a very over-sized car by a white-gloved chauffeur, the kind of arrangement I remembered only from films of the thirties. One early evening, when we were returned from our chores of the day, we decided to venture outside the walls by ourselves. As we walked we carefully plotted our excursion, noting landmarks much in the way that, in childhood tales, one would leave a trail to return on. As we walked we took notice of a light here, an odd-shaped sign there, an ornamented wall on a street beyond. Now, outside our grounds and three blocks to the left, we came upon a wide, busy avenue full of cars, shops, and people bustling about. On one corner was a large *pachinko* gambling house, filled mostly with men in their thirties and forties looking very proper in their dark business suits. On the other corner were the recognizable golden arches of McDonald's. Many of the shops and boutiques were filled with young, attractive, well-groomed people. In the States I suppose we would refer to them as "yuppies."

The street, the name of which we never found out, ran a long way, a little like Broadway, with huge blinking neon signs in wild, loud, and garish colors. It was very exciting to the eyes, all the brilliant reds, yellows, blues, and greens, all in Japanese characters and totally unintelligible to us. We guessed they announced restaurants, bars, cinemas, etc. We didn't know. Somewhat overwhelmed after a while, we happily retraced our steps.

The next afternoon, finding myself alone and having been told by the hotel clerk that I could buy an English-language newspaper only a few blocks away, I ventured out. It was a glorious, sunny day, the first such in the week since we had arrived. Outside the gate, as I turned this time to the right, I saw an area that looked quite different from the one we had walked about in. It looked to be only a few blocks away. Humming to myself, I sallied forth. I breathed the fragrant air and thought to myself, "This is more like it!" I didn't ask, "like what?"

After several blocks the streets began to become quite narrow, and the brick and stucco buildings, five or so stories high, had the look of post-Second-World-War structures. They seemed to be apartment houses, spotted with entries into the buildings. Most had shops along the street level. I looked into a corner hardware store, then another store that seemed to be a shoe-repair or leatherware shop, and a tea shop, perhaps? All of these, cheek by jowl, were filled with people—some couples and several women pushing baby carts or carrying their babies in small kangaroo-style pouches while juggling packages in their arms. There were older men and women too, though the lack of gray in the uniformly black heads made it difficult for me to guess what their actual ages might be. They all moved about into the shops, onto the streets, darting back and forth between the slow-moving cars. The narrow sidewalks were of course too narrow to accommodate them all. Ah! I finally understood, this was a neighborhood. Indeed, this was more "like it."

Though I had already walked a number of blocks, I hadn't yet found what I thought might be a newspaper stand or a paper and magazine and candy shop that would carry newspapers. But from the corner of my eye, as I was about to pass it by, I saw what the English would call a greengrocer. The shop was surely no larger than about five feet wide and fifteen deep. Yet it had a small center aisle and was filled waist-high with neatly placed fruits and vegetables in bins beginning at the back wall of the shop and overflowing onto the sidewalk.

There I came to an abrupt halt. Because we had been served only frozen orange juice since we arrived in Japan, my California eyes zeroed in on a wonderfully balanced stack of hand-woven brown straw baskets, each containing five fantastic-looking oranges, against one wall of the shop and coming out to just about where I had stopped. There was a little cardboard sign sitting in the topmost basket with a number on it, surprisingly a recognizable number, and quite large. I assumed that it was the price of the basket in yen. The amount was definitely too high to be the cost of a single item. I, thinking quizzically "Why five oranges?" wondered if that was the number required to make up the specified weight for the price. Or did it have something to do with the fact that, like the number thirteen for us, four is thought to be an unlucky number in Japan, as I had been told. I picked out only two oranges and fumbled in my purse for some yen. Dividing by five made my arithmetic struggle as I tried to work out the cost of two. I took out more yen than my poor mathematics called for—just in case.

Coming down the aisle from the back of the shop with a shuffling sound from the backless straw slippers he wore, a white-haired little old man, bent with age, moved in my direction. He wore a spotless white apron that matched his hair. His narrow black eyes glistened, his cheeks had a pinkish glow, and his smile, with too many teeth for a man his age, went from ear to ear. He came within two feet of me, looked straight into my eyes, and uttered a stream of sound, very song-like but unintelligible to me—except for the one Japanese word, "Hi," which I was always able to single out.

I stiffened, clutching my two oranges to me in my left hand, and, with my broadest smile, raised my right hand, showing two fingers in the typical "V" for victory sign, and placed the yen in his hand. Without a sound he scurried back up the aisle to the register and returned with, and placed, a lovely yellow grapefruit in the arm with the oranges. Our smiles remained as I returned the grapefruit to him with one hand and with the other rubbed my thumb and index finger together vigorously, a gesture I remember seeing in an old Italian film where the sign meant money. I again heard "Hi…" as he scrambled up the aisle. This time he returned with a few coins, which he placed in one of my hands while he grabbed an orange from the other. I was beginning to feel frustrated when he turned to me again with two oranges and, after inspecting them very carefully, placed into my hand the more luscious one—not the one he had taken back. Our smiles never stopped.

With that done, he stepped back and bent to the waist in my direction. I returned the gesture, bending half over and toward him as if he were the rising sun. He hadn't moved away, and then bowed again. Still smiling, down I went, this time low enough so that my nose touched the asparagus tips stacked in front of me. I heard a chuckle from behind and, though being unable to move while the little man was bobbing up and down, my eyes caught sight of a number of people who had stopped to witness our little exchange. This time panic set in. With what I imagined to be approaching my tenth bow in a seemingly unending sequence, I stood absolutely erect, raised my right hand at the elbow, bent my four fingers twice, and, in what was more a grin than a smile, I said, "Bye-bye!" and turned a ninety-degree angle and walked away.

When I reentered the hotel, the clerk at the desk noticed my oranges and inquired if I had purchased a newspaper as well. I shook my head, "No." He replied, "Too bad, the paper stand is only a few steps away from where you shopped."

On our last day in Tokyo, I was determined to find a newspaper I could read. And so I did. I had started to return to the hotel when I once again came upon the fruit-and-vegetable store. The little man, now with his back toward me, was handing something to a couple who were definitely speaking the King's English to each other. To my utter surprise I also could very clearly hear "Bye-bye!" As I walked by the little man, I felt a small tug at my sleeve. He backed up, stood erect, bent his arm at the elbow, waved his fingers at me, and with the broadest smile I have ever seen, said, "Bye-bye!"—and with his other hand placed an orange in the pocket of my raincoat. I turned toward the sun, made my deepest bow, and went on my way.

While walking back and fingering the orange, I thought of Shakespeare's words, "All the world's a stage." What, I wondered, would he have made of these scenes?

Topkapi and Me

Topkapi and Me

In 1989 my husband went to Turkey to lecture on English literature. I accompanied him. Our first stop was Istanbul, an exotic city of domes and minarets and the look of the East. And, of course, we visited the great Topkapi Palace museum. There I was somewhat overwhelmed when, as I stood looking in one of the display windows, the guard standing in front of it announced to a multitude of people, and in several languages (one of the them being perfect English), "You are looking at the largest diamond in the world: eighty carats."

It sat rather primly propped up on a cloth. I was a bit disappointed: it did not look overly faceted and gave off a somewhat yellow glow. In Topkapi there were also many rooms of bejeweled thrones, sabers, bowls, cups, and such things. As I looked at them all I became determined that I would not leave this country without something to decorate me. I later went for several hours to the famous covered shopping bazaar and searched through the many stalls, but I was overcome by their endless number and by the crowds that filled the place. It wasn't to be in Istanbul.

Our next stop was Ankara, the capital of Turkey, which was looked down upon as the second city and for its newness and lack of sophistication. The city is a two-hour plane ride from Istanbul and is situated on a series of hills in the midst of a great wide flat plain. The buildings were mostly built in the 1930s and 1940s. There were the president's estate on a hill, the embassies, apartment buildings on large, tree-lined avenues, and what looked like a downtown shopping area in a mid-sized midwestern city at home.

After Istanbul, this did seem a drab place. Yet I was to find that everything about the place was marked by sharp contrasts. I came to be deeply affected by them. The city park has a Greek theater built of stones that date back to ancient Greece. There, performances are given all summer long. One new hilltop shopping mall has a restaurant that is built on top of a structure that strongly resembles the Seattle space-needle.

There is also the Anatolian Museum, a treasure in itself, totally modern inside, but with Hittite pieces dating back over six thousand years, and placed inside a fourteenth-century mosque. The museum was on a high hill next to some walls that are the remains of a medieval fort. Within these walls are stone houses of old Ankara, where I could see Turkish women, in their regional dress with colorful aprons and covered heads, hanging clothes, beating rugs, or shodding peas, in front of the open heavy wooden doors.

Once inside the walls, I followed my nose to an open door. The smell of freshly baked bread drew me near. Inside I saw a woman baking breads in a wood-burning oven of stones and mortar, while her child pulled them gently out with a long-handled wooden paddle and carefully placed the golden brown loaves on a cloth on the earthen floor of their house. I was sure I was witnessing a ritual that has been repeated in the same manner for hundreds of years.

For me the most amusing part of that little excursion, one that reinforced my sense of strange contrasts, occurred when the young Turkish student who accompanied me pointed to the top of the hill where there was an imposing sign that she said displayed the name of a restaurant up there. Originally built in the sixth century, it had, she said, once been the home of a wealthy Turkish merchant. It resembled a large wooden lodge and must have had a commanding view of the entire valley. For its age it had a surprising number of stories, and outside the top floor I could see that a small deck had been built, on which were placed some chairs and a wooden table. In the center of the table a brilliant red umbrella had been positioned. On it were written the words "Coca-Cola."

Our first night out (as well as many others), away from official dinners, we spent with Seyfi Doltas, a teacher at Hacettype University, who about ten years before, when he was studying for a graduate degree in English, had been in classes taught by my husband. He had requested that he be our guide and met us at dinner time in the lobby of the Hilton hotel. A slightly built man in his early forties, he had black hair, a moustache, and twinkling black eyes. He wore a dark suit, a lightly wrinkled white shirt with a tie somewhat askew, and very polished shoes, though turned out at the heels. In the back of his jacket sleeve there was a small tear that never was repaired in the many times we met him. He had a wonderful smile and a sharp and disarming wit that we discovered as time went on.

"Greetings!" he said, "I see they have put you in the pink palace!"

"Ah! Seyfi," my husband replied, "you haven't changed a bit," to which he answered, "*Merci*," (the French word for "thank you"), which was the end word whenever anyone answered us in Turkish or English. The people we encountered, teachers and merchants alike, seemed to be under the illusion that French was the international language and that *"Merci"* was the proper polite response.

And Seyfi was correct. The Hilton was all pink marble with crystal chandeliers. It had buffet breakfasts with bacon and pancakes and a very Western-style restaurant that served American and Continental food. Seyfi was clearly uncomfortable there. He did, however, accept a drink in the bar as we exchanged pleasantries and information about people we knew in common. We learned that he was married and had a daughter, and though he wrote his articles by hand and used the University typewriter in his office, his cousin, during a short trip to England, had bought him a used computer with limited, simple software, and Seyfi was teaching his daughter to use it. We also learned that he did not own a car and, uncommon as it was in families like his, his wife, Elem, worked.

When we finished our drink, he inquired, "What is your pleasure?" My husband and I replied in unison, "A Turkish meal." I followed by asking, "How shall we go?"

"By taxi, always taxis!" he responded. But every evening, after saying "Good night," I saw him head out the hotel door straight for the taxi stand, but then make a sharp left turn down the street and disappear. We never inquired, but I strongly suspected Seyfi never took a taxi and instead simply walked the several miles to his home or, when it was not too late at night, took one of the always over-crowded buses that ran at the end of the street. There, abutting the property of the hotel, was the Iranian embassy, with its bigger-than-life portrait of Ayatollah Khomeini hanging on the face of the building. The embassy had enormous black gates, which seemed to be neither guarded nor open whenever we rode by. During our many discussions about Turkey, Seyfi spoke with fear about fundamentalism and its influence. In describing the struggles of his troubled country, he kept insisting with approval that it had been trying very hard to look toward the West. I shudder to think how difficult it must have been for him to walk by that embassy.

Seyfi did take us to a Turkish restaurant. It was in what he referred to as "restaurant row," a large open mall with fountains. Because it was May and the weather was mild, the restaurant we went to had set out wooden picnic tables and benches with colorful cloths on an open-air patio marked out by potted ferns. There were some couples and families seated at the tables. But I inquired why we had also seen tables of young men drinking together and even eating together. Seyfi simply answered, "Young women of their age do not go out unescorted by their elders unless they are engaged."

The meal was an experience. Since we were not at all conversant with the Turkish language, he explained that the meal had three parts: appetizers, main dish, and "perhaps" dessert. We soon learned what "perhaps" meant. The first course came in as many varieties as we wished to consume: small dishes filled with bits of meats, fish, and vegetables, (some, like eggplant, we could easily identify), but mostly they were wonderful mixtures of herbs and spices, some very delicate and others strong in flavor. The abundance of the food, its quality and flavors, was indescribable. In fact, when we came to the main dish of a magnificently presented fish on a bed of fresh vegetables, we could only make a slight attempt at getting it down. Seyfi explained to our very solicitous but quizzical waiter that we were doing this for the first time and there was no problem with the food. The waiter beamed and appeared with a tray of fresh white almonds. The mound looked as if it was two feet high. At the side of the tray was a small scale, and with a deft movement he scooped up a small amount of nuts in a metal cup, put them on the scale to be weighed, and then emptied them into three small dishes and placed one in front of each of us. This was dessert—superb!

Since I still intended to find some ornament for myself and Seyfi could not help me, it was an American woman working for the United States Information Agency who told me where best to buy my jewelry. She sent me to an arcade only a short distance on foot from the hotel, and made me a walking map that I followed step by step. The arcade was a long, underground corridor below several business buildings. Both sides of the walkway were lined with shops stuffed beyond imagination with jewelry, silver, clothes, rugs, and anything else one could think of in the line of gifts. At first look I was a little intimidated. As I carefully maneuvered about the center while glancing from left to right, I noticed that many of the shops had little signs in the windows saying "English spoken here" or "*Ici on parle Français*," with Visa or Mastercard symbols as well. Most of the time, when there was no customer in any one of these small, overstuffed shops, the shopkeeper stood in the doorway, and when someone looked at the show-window, he would smile broadly, point at the object, and beckon the looker to enter the shop. This apparently was standard procedure.

I finally paused at a shop. It was filled from ceiling to floor with ornate silver tea-sets, platters, dishes, anything one can imagine that can be produced in silver. But one window that displayed several trays of necklaces, bracelets, pins, and earrings caught my fancy. As I walked toward the window, a single necklace struck a familiar chord. A charming young man, perhaps in his thirties, pranced out toward me, beckoned, and I entered. He had gone to a British school, and in a lovely English he engaged me in conversation and brought to the counter several of the trays to which I had pointed. Since he had learned from our conversation that I was an artist, he told me I had a discerning eye when I had picked out the topaz-colored necklace. It consisted of six strands of beads held together with carved silver pieces, and a circular centerpiece of wrought silver that held a small, faceted, and pronged topaz. It was, he said, a fine copy of a nineteenth-century Turkish necklace in the Topkapi museum.

When some people entered the store, he left for a moment and reappeared with a leather stool and asked me to be seated. I obliged. After he and the new customers had completed their business, he disappeared again and reappeared with a beautiful silver tray holding a handsome teapot and two small porcelain cups enrobed in carved silver holders. We drank tea. I learned that his father had been a silversmith and had owned the shop before him. He too enjoyed working in silver, but mainly as a hobby. Indeed, when I admired several silver pins, he admitted that he had made them and added that they were designs taken from the Hittite collection in the Anatolian museum.

I noticed that over an hour had passed much too quickly. We bargained a little over the necklace (only because I was told it was impolite not to do so) before we agreed on a price. As he was wrapping my package and I was preparing to leave, I took out my lipstick, which has a small mirror attached to it. Watching me, he commented, "Very tricky, but not *très élégant*." We exchanged cards and shook hands, and he handed me my package and the receipt for customs. As I started to depart from the store, he handed me a second wrapped package and said, "With my compliments and my pleasure."

When I returned home, I was very excited to open my purchase. I did, and put it on at once. When I went on to open the second package, my gift, I found, encased in a silver backing and frame, a mirror large enough to fit in the palm of my hand. I put it in my purse.

Unhappily, when I wore the necklace again, the prong on the center stone caught on my coat collar and pulled the stone loose. So I took the necklace to my local jeweler to be repaired. He looked at it, and then at me, and shrugged, saying, "You must be aware that your necklace is all glass and poor silver—almost not worth the bother." Though I was dismayed, I still insisted he bother. Then in my open purse he saw the mirror and said, "Let me see that." He took it, examined it closely, and said earnestly, "The mirror is in bad shape and worn. You must let me replace it for you. The wrought silver backing is quite elegant. I haven't seen anything like it in years. It certainly is rare, and I would not be surprised if it is a valuable antique."

India—Side by Side

India—Side by Side

As I open the neat shoe-box-sized package, wrapped in cheesecloth and secured with red sealing wax, undamaged even though it has been six months in traveling from India, my thoughts go immediately back to what have surely been several of the most puzzling and mysterious moments of my life.

It was in the winter of 1984 that my husband, who had spent three years in India during the Second World War with a unit engaged in breaking Japanese code, had an opportunity to return to India. He had long felt the need to show me "his India" and had many times throughout our long marriage promised to do so. Having now received several invitations to lecture at a number of universities there, he said, "We have waited too long for you to come with me to that fascinating country. And now is the time." And indeed we did go.

On one of our memorable stops we arrived at the Hotel Banjara in the city of Hyderabad. I had been told that under the "British raj" it had been the capital of one of what had been called the "princely states" and had been forced to become part of India when that country achieved independence. The evidence of its peculiar status as a Moslem "princely state" was still visible in the odd look of the slate-colored, onion-domed tombs on the horizon at the outskirts of the city. Our hotel was a short way out of town. It was a large, square brick building about six stories high, with the modern look of a structure built in the thirties that had been refurbished many times. I was told that, before the Indian liberation from England, it was placed there to be close to a British cantonment in order to serve English families and foreign visitors. Now it mainly accommodates tourists. The hotel looked out over a flat plain on one side; on the other side it sat next to a pond about the size of a football field.

Every morning of the week we spent there we had breakfast on a small patio on the side of the hotel overlooking the pond. Our meal, hardly native, consisted of fresh-squeezed orange juice, a platter of pineapple, mangoes, and bananas, heated French imported croissants, and a variety of rolls and toasts and freshly brewed coffee. And every morning, as I was sipping the last of my coffee and finishing my continental fare, my eyes wandered across the pond to the first of a series of thatched-roof huts that faced in my direction. A small native village, I thought.

I had seen only one other similar collection of huts when we stayed at a hotel south of Madras on the Bay of Bengal. That group of huts was situated just south of the hotel property, which was enclosed by a chain-link fence with an Indian guard standing foursquare in front of it. One afternoon back then, while sunning myself quite close to the fence, I suddenly heard voices and looked up to see a group of the villagers emerging from their huts and gathering in a large huddle on the beach. There seemed to be a great deal of chattering and excitement among both children and adults. I was overcome with curiosity. I approached the guard, who happily understood and spoke English. When I asked what was going on, he replied, "This happens once every week about this time. Watch the horizon."

I gazed out to sea and I could see two boats with two black sails coming swiftly toward the shore. As they approached, the din became even louder. The boats were then beached, and on what I thought might have been a sail cloth were placed a large number of fish in separate piles. The men of the village approached, and a very heated exchange began between them and the fishermen. There was no doubt in my mind that they were auctioning off the fish. Within not more than fifteen minutes the villagers had gathered up their fish and were gone from the beach almost without a sound, as quickly as they had appeared. Looking out at the sea, I could see the two black sails disappearing over the horizon.

The little village across the pond in Hyderabad held something of that same mystery and fascination for me. Every morning I watched the thatched hut facing me that was closest to the pond. It had a single door, and a ditch and fire pit dug in front of it. I did not perceive any windows. And every morning as I watched, the door opened and out came a man, a woman, a little boy, a dog, a chicken, and a water buffalo, all except the chicken proceeding directly into the water, the color of which, from our side, tended to be more brown than blue. The sounds of splashing and romping came across to us. And they disappeared back into the hut before we left our table.

How I longed to be able to cross the distance that separated the two sides of the pond, or at least to make some contact with that far-off world which was suddenly so strangely close. I spotted a baseball-sized, bright yellow sponge ball in the shop of the hotel. I had seen two little English girls playing with one on the back lawn. I purchased it, and at breakfast the next morning I made my husband, to his great embarrassment, wind up his baseball arm and pitch it in the direction of the little boy in the water on the other side. It fell into the pond and seemed to be floating in his direction. Did I only imagine that he looked at it, and then at me? But he and the family disappeared, as on the day before, almost without a sound.

The next morning, our last, the same scene of the appearance of the family and animals repeated itself on schedule. I never spotted the yellow ball. But as we were about to depart, to the left of my foot, floating on the pond, very close to where we were sitting, was a little wooden boat. It was delicately hand-carved and about five inches in length, with a very carefully shaved and shaped piece of wood for the sail. We were alone on the terrace and the group in the pond had disappeared. I knew it was for me. So I seized it and later mailed it home with my other Indian souvenirs.

Bombay was our last stop before returning home. It was there, in the Jehangir Art Gallery, that I sensed again the crossing of the line to this untouchable and yet so closely related ancient world. The gallery was showing a remarkable group of paintings done by the "Warlis," the people of a small, remote village. Their paintings of village life were done on the walls of their huts, which had first been smeared with dung. When dried it gave the wall a very deep brownish-gray color. The wall was then painted on with a single reed dipped in a thick, pure white mixture of rice water.

A European artist had accidentally come upon the village, and while visiting the huts was so struck by the beauty, sophistication, and quality of the work that he brought it to the attention of Mr. Gandhi, the owner of the Jehangir Art Gallery, who returned to the village with him. When he saw the painted walls, he agreed that they were impressive—and as contemporary as the work of an artist like Trova. Mr. Gandhi later arranged for this exhibit of the villagers' work in his Bombay gallery. I responded with a strange warmth and even understanding to these representations, at once naive in style and masterful in execution, of the details of daily activities of the village as well as the precise renderings of its natural environment.

Of course, I did not buy any of the paintings displayed in the gallery. They were, unfortunately, too expensive. The reason for their high cost, I imagine, very few people would be able to guess. Mr. Gandhi explained it to me. Since they were originally painted on the walls and could not be removed for display and sale in a gallery, he sent paper for the villager-artists to work on. But when the finished paintings were returned, the odor of dung was so strong that they had to be encased in air-tight plastic frames before they could be hung. All this was a procedure as extravagant as it was unusual. I, of course, bought only an illustrated catalog of the exhibit.

Now, having finished unpacking the precious cargo of the cheesecloth package, I sit at the window of my tenth-floor Los Angeles apartment, vintage 1990, and look at the high-rise building opposite, on the other side of a space I have no desire to cross, since that building is only a reflection of my own. Some people come out of an apartment onto a deck, but they do not capture my attention. As I take out my catalog and little wooden boat and place them on my modern mirrored mantelpiece, I cannot help but wonder how often even a casual look at them will evoke those moments of exotic exchange—the slight and yet almost miraculous spanning of an unbridgeable gap.

The Refrigerator—
"Silence Absolu"

The Refrigerator—
"Silence Absolu"

I arrived back in Paris on a glorious Easter Sunday morning in the spring of 1988, the kind of spring that only this city could produce after a gray, dark, cold, and rainy winter. I had been in London for several days, researching some materials in the Warburg Library to be used in the artwork I was doing for a textbook. My husband was a lecturer at the Sorbonne for the year, and we were settled in a splendid four-room apartment in a building erected after the Second World War, but totally modernized: we had white leather furniture in the living room, a marble bathroom right down to the bidet, and a kitchen that had not only a sixteen-cubic-foot, two-door refrigerator-freezer, but an instant coffee-maker, Cuisinart, and almost every other gadget one could think of.

When, thirsty from the trip, I opened the refrigerator door, to my utter surprise a warm, sour, waft of air came at me. Of course, the freezer, which had been filled to the brim, was a soggy mess. I jiggled the dials and then pulled the plug from the wall. As I was playing with the plug, I noticed a package on the table nearby, with a note attached. It was from my next-door neighbor, an undaunted-by-anything

American. It said, "Hi, J. The *concierge* let me in. Our husbands are sailing their paper boats in the park. I've left you some croissants and a thermos of coffee. There was an unannounced strike and we haven't had any electricity since Saturday. Come join us! Fix things later. See you. R."

"Oh my—doesn't that ring a bell!" I thought to myself. And I couldn't resist sitting down and thinking way back to our first Easter Sunday in Paris.

It was the week before Easter Sunday in 1958 when we—my husband, my four-year old daughter, and I—arrived from England to the Paris of thirty years ago for a stay of six months. My husband was on sabbatical leave from his university, and we had spent six months in England and were now coming to France for him to complete the research for his next book. Rental apartments were almost impossible to come by, especially for families with children. In desperation, while still in a hotel we appealed to a dear French friend we had come to know quite well when he was a graduate student in the U.S. And with 50,000 francs (then a bit over $100) paid under the table, he negotiated and outbid the Russian embassy for a three-room apartment at 17 rue de Chazelles, only three blocks from where we would be living thirty years later.

The apartment was in a turn-of-the-century building five stories high. It had a large circular wooden staircase and two apartments on each floor. The *patron,* or owner, lived on the top floor, and there was no elevator. Our apartment faced the street and was on the ground floor (*rez-de-chaussée*), which was not considered desirable. Our entry door was next to that of the caretaker of the building (*concierge*). Except for us, all the families in the building were French; ours was the only apartment rented to foreigners. Mme. Mougèle, the *concierge*, showed us through the apartment and gave us our keys. There was a small bedroom, a large living room with a carved marble fireplace and a sleeping couch, a large dining room with another fireplace, a bathroom (tub), a W.C., and a closet-sized room that was the kitchen. The furnishings were all dog-eared Empire style. The closet-size kitchen had a sink, which was only large enough to hold a single cooking-pot, and a two-burner gas stove with an oven no deeper than twelve inches. It had two small hanging cupboards with dishes in them. On the wall hung four flints for lighting the stove. They were made with beautifully wrought handles of wood, marble, glass, and stone. I reminded myself that back home one small pilot light was sufficient even for my old-fashioned stove.

Happily, my college French stood me in good stead as Mme. Mougèle, rotund and rather gruff, unsmilingly informed us that she had never had any children in the building before. She told me her husband worked for an automobile corporation as a mechanic and her only son was a house-painter. We learned later that she had grown up in the mountains of the Vosges and had been in the underground during the Second World War. We also discovered before we left Paris that her secret desire was to own a pair of white, beaded-leather Indian moccasins. Later, upon our return to our home in Minnesota, we easily found and sent her a pair of them. One of the people in the building wrote us in a Christmas letter the following year that they remained on her feet until they were in shreds.

Until Mme. Mougèle first handed us the keys to the apartment, my daughter followed us around without a sound. Once inside, she suddenly tugged at my dress and asked "Mommy, where is the refrigerator?" When Madame, as we later referred to her, heard the word, she immediately replied that those foreigners who required a refrigerator usually rented one and put it in the dining room. It then occurred to me that ours was the front half of what had been a large apartment, and the Mougèles, with the back half, had the kitchen. With her statement about the refrigerator, she patted my daughter on the head and fingered her shoulder-length brown curls—which I must admit had been admired by others—and *sotto voce* said *"poupée"* ("doll"). My daughter, not knowing one word of French, immediately translated it to be her name, said it loudly twice, came up with a gigantic smile and a hug around the large frame of Madame, and disappeared into the bedroom. I could tell it was love at first sight, as it certainly proved to be. From then on my daughter was known only by the name "Poupée".

Of course we felt we needed a refrigerator, and a typewriter as well, and as there was a rental shop within a few blocks, it became the job of my husband to procure them. On the Monday afternoon of our arrival he returned with a typewriter and a rental contract for an eight-cubic-foot, two-door refrigerator freezer to be delivered, as they told him, *"Cet après midi, ou au plus tard demain matin!"* ("This afternoon, or at the very latest tomorrow morning").

On Tuesday morning I opened the metal shutters of the living-room windows facing the street, and there, parked at the front door, was a small blue panel truck with nothing less than a sparkling white refrigerator at least twelve cubic feet in size, being lowered from it. My daughter and Madame were already standing hand-in-hand in the hall, together with a neighbor who quietly asked if perhaps she might be permitted to put a small piece of meat in it sometime, as she had done once before when a previous tenant had gotten so splendid an appliance. I beamed *"avec plaisir"* with joy and excitement, for suddenly the refrigerator had taken on the aura of a rare acquisition. The delivery man placed it in a corner of the dining room and connected the plug. It made a strange growling noise. He adjusted some knobs and tried again. But it was even louder. He took off the front panel and began unscrewing the motor. When I asked what the problem was, he replied that he didn't know but would send the motor to be repaired and expected it to be back in four to six weeks. In shock I insisted that this would not do and that he had to return the refrigerator to the store at once. And he did.

That afternoon my husband went back to the rental store and was told that there would be no problem if we would accept a slightly smaller refrigerator they had in the store. He of course acceded and was promised delivery "this afternoon, or the very latest tomorrow morning."

All afternoon our door remained open, and I managed to meet most of the people in our building. I realized why when I saw my daughter standing in our doorway and greeting everyone who came in, man or woman, by saying *"Bonjour, Madame.* I am Poupée, American. Our refrigerator is coming. This is my mother." Having lived all of her life in a single-family dwelling, she found this to be a great adventure. She followed Mme. Mougèle around like a puppy, chattering incessantly in English and imitating whatever words of French she could pick up. (In time the French would come quickly, as twice a day she zipped onto Mme. Mougèle's lap and handed her a hairbrush with which to brush her curls—a ritual that Madame performed lovingly—while they listened to the transatlantic radio together.)

Meanwhile Wednesday came and went with no refrigerator. So I telephoned and was again reassured. In the morning the blue panel truck was greeted by several people from their windows. This time it held a single-door refrigerator a few cubic feet smaller than the first one. The same delivery man brought it in. And once again he placed it in its proper place and was about to plug it in when, looking troubled, he asked if I had a large scissor. He explained that the plug was too large for the outlet—the plug was huge—and so he wanted to cut it off and replace it with a smaller one he had in the truck. Stunned by the bizarre suggestion, I suddenly had a vision of a grand explosion. Trying to remain calm, I immediately said, *"Pas possible!"* and back he and the refrigerator went.

Friday (good Friday) it was I who went to the store and told my tale of woe to the secretary of the owner, who seemed to take pity on me. She said the *patron* had just bought a new refrigerator and would be very happy to rent his old one to us. Of course, she said, it was a bit smaller, but a very reliable French-made one. I again agreed. She told me it would arrive on Friday afternoon—or at the very latest on Saturday morning.

Not Saturday morning, but afternoon, the blue truck once more came chugging down the street, with a greeting from half the people he passed. The delivery man unloaded, to my pure amazement, a refrigerator the size of a block of ice. He had a grin from ear to ear as he attached it to the wall and said that we would no longer have any problems, since this refrigerator worked on the principle of "absorption." It had no motor and provided *"silence absolu."* He was absolutely correct. We calculated that by American standards it was about four cubic feet in size, and by Easter Sunday morning it had managed to produce four small, not altogether solid, ice cubes. On that glorious sunny day we went to the Tuileries to watch the children sail their boats on the pond. Since we could store nothing safely at home, we had a lovely meal out. In my mind I resigned myself to do my three-times-a-day shopping starting Monday, as Mme. Mougèle had earlier intimated the French so sensibly did.

And here I was, thirty years later, preparing to do the same, once more on the Monday after Easter, after I had picked up the phone and called to inquire about the power shortage. I suppose I should have guessed at the outcome when I heard a very reassuring voice from the other end. It was a taped message, saying, "Please do not disturb yourself, Madame or Monsieur. The electricity will be turned on tomorrow afternoon, or at the very latest Tuesday morning" (English translation).

Paris, still Paris—I held the phone in my hand in absolute silence.

Encore Paris

Encore Paris

It was June of 1953 and close to our fifth wedding anniversary. My husband and I were living, quite modestly, on our first extended stay in Paris. Our neighbors in our apartment building had become very close friends over a period of only a few months. My husband and I were American teachers, and Don and Ann were Canadians working for their government. We found we had many things in common, even our wedding anniversaries—the same day and year. So of course we decided to celebrate together.

All of us were childless at the time, but as a foursome we were a rather staid, serious, and thoughtful group. This night, however, we decided to be a bit carefree and celebrate at what we had heard was a typical French restaurant with entertainment, not too expensive but, we hoped, allowing for an occasion to remember. It certainly was that.

The restaurant was called A la Bonne Franquette and was situated on a large square in the Montmartre section. It was one of several restaurants that shared the square. All of them had an enclosed area but also had seating opening onto the square. The outside tables were set under large trees that were decorated with colored lights. Of the several restaurants sitting side by side, A La Bonne Franquette was the first on the corner leading onto the square.

We were seated at a table in the outdoor area. The moon was full, the air was soft and warm, and the four of us, already entranced, decided in advance that although we had taken the metro there, we would splurge and take a taxi back.

Our waiter, Georges, remarked that we seemed a particularly smiling group. When we told why we were celebrating, he rubbed his hands and said, *"O, la, la—c'est spécial!"* He whispered something in our husbands' ears, they nodded, and in a flash Georges reappeared with a bottle of champagne. It was about eight o'clock and the place was very quickly beginning to fill up. Georges said he was exclusively ours for the evening as he danced up to the table with a variety of *hors d'oeuvres* to accompany our drinks. He informed us that the entertainment, a pianist and an accordionist, began at nine, in the garden area.

We never saw a menu. Georges declared with bravado that he was in total charge. We had a mixed green salad, and as we began our main dish, which was a *steack au poivre* with *dauphiné* potatoes and green peas, the music began. Georges suddenly appeared with a very potable bottle of red wine (compliments of the chef, he said), humming as he poured.

The musicians played songs we knew and songs we didn't know. The chief entertainer, an accordionist-singer-master-of-ceremonies, came to our table, pulled over a chair and sat down, and taught us a drinking song. He asked us our names and where we came from, lingered and laughed with us. He encouraged us to dance and sing, to sing loudly. We even joined with the people at the next table, who we were told were Australians, exchanging warm greetings with them as with old friends. We were deliriously happy.

For each of us the dessert was a flaming ice cream ball, and all the restaurant, led by the accordionist seconded by Georges, stood to sing "Happy Anniversary." When the bill was paid (not beyond our modest budget, we were told by our grateful spouses), Georges hugged and kissed us all and gave Ann and me each a rose. As we left, the accordionist wildly gestured "goodbye" and sang a farewell song that followed us out. We waltzed over to a taxi and declared this to have been one of the happiest nights of all our lives.

Five years later it was our good fortune to be in Paris in June for a teachers' conference, which was taking place during the week of our tenth anniversary. It seemed too perfect not to return to A la Bonne Franquette (of course, provided it was still in business) even though our friends would not be there to join us. We had planned to send them a telegram greeting from Paris, but now we could look forward to adding to it, describing a joyous return to our special place. We consulted the phone book and discovered with excitement that it was still there.

On the evening of our anniversary, dressed in what I judged to be our finest, we sneaked away from the conference group, and, telling no one of our plans, we took off for Montmartre, this time by taxi. Everything augured well for our return. Again it was a moonlit, balmy evening, and I could sense we both felt as if we were under the spell of the night and of our special history. Again it was a bit early, and as we stepped out of the taxi we could see that many of the tables of all the restaurants were still quite empty.

The *Maitre d'* approached us, but without any explanation to him, we chose a table in the open area, not too far, we decided, from the table we had had before. A very pleasant-looking waiter approached us and asked if we had been there before. We both gave a very knowing nod. He then asked if we would like the *table d'hôte* (a five-course set meal) or the *à la carte* menu. Feeling very sophisticated and very expansive—thinking, who knows what this night will bring?—we ordered champagne cocktails and one ounce of caviar. The price was forbidding, the residue of our conservativism reminded us, but we felt reassured since the caviar was to be weighed at the table. We toasted each other exuberantly, responding to a wonderful feeling of butterflies in the stomach.

The table next to us, we noticed, was filling up with a cheerful group of six who were unmistakably British. While they settled in, (we saw that they were not given menus), their waiter served them champagne and *hors d'oeuvres*, and moved about in a way that seemed very familiar to us. On our side we had a salad of mixed greens and walnuts in a delicate dressing.

The music began. It was a pianist (an older woman) and an accordionist (a lively young man) performing on a wooden dance floor set on the ground in the midst of the tables. Our waiter had suggested a veal dish (a specialty of the chef) and an appropriate fine wine. As we were about to drink our Châteauneuf-du-Pape, I watched while the waiter at the next table, with a great flourish, produced a bottle of wine much like the one we had drunk five years before, to accompany what appeared to be their *steacks au poivre*. Because he spoke loudly enough, we heard him say that it was sent with the compliments of the chef as a gesture to their birthday celebration. When I asked our waiter whether the chef often sends out a complimentary bottle of wine, he answered, somewhat archly, "If they had looked at the menu, they would have seen that a bottle of *vin rouge ordinaire* is always included in the basic *table d'hôte* dinner. As we ate we heard the music and the singing become louder, and we watched as the accordionist went over to the next table and began teaching them the chorus and words of the drinking song we still remembered. The fluttering of the butterflies slowed to a stop.

We ordered a finely made apple tart for dessert, while in came the flaming ice cream balls to the other table. We even got up to sing happy birthday to the special person at the neighboring table, and we all shook hands while their waiter, rose in hand, hugged and kissed the birthday girl. Sitting down again to our own twosome, my husband and I toasted each other over a final cognac (*Fine Champagne*) and agreed on the quality of our meal. However, we decided not to mention our little nostalgic trip to our Canadian friends when we sent our greetings to them. Wasn't it Thomas Wolfe who said, "You can't go home again," we mused?

We really never had! It was one month later, when we were checking through our foreign expenses that had been put on our credit card, that we discovered that our extravagant bill for that night came from La Fromentière, not A la Bonne Franquette. We had been sitting and dining in the restaurant next door.

Germany—*"Natürlich"*

Germany—*"Natürlich"*

When we arrived for the third time at our apartment on Eichhornstrasse, I was prepared. I had a box of candles, four yellow light bulbs, and one spray-can of OFF. It was the third consecutive July we would spend in Konstanz, a small city on the largest lake in Germany. Three years ago my husband had first been asked to deliver a series of lectures there at the University of Konstanz. This campus of the German university system had opened in the mid-1960s, at much the same time as the younger campuses of the University of California. Los Angeles, seat of one of the older campuses, was our home.

Our hosts in the Department of Literature had then arranged for us to rent a severely modern (Bauhaus style) apartment in a heavily ornate Jugendstil building (circa 1910), which had been redone to accommodate visitors at the university. Konstanz was in large part a Renaissance city, though with a nineteenth-century atmosphere. In architecture it ran the gamut from medieval to postmodern. All around the city was the picturesque lake with an esplanade where people strolled under beautifully kept and carefully trimmed rows of plane trees and looked toward the Swiss mountains in the distance.

We had some access to this impressive view. Thanks to a large deck that was part of our second-floor apartment, we could see part of the lake, only one street away. The apartment, which gave the impression of a black-and-white photograph, was transformed by the colorful fresh flowers I brought home from the open-air street market every Tuesday and Saturday. On other days I tried to meet my household needs at a somewhat drab German version of an American-style indoor mall.

On our first July 4th we asked our university hosts, a couple with whom we very quickly became friendly, to have dinner with us. Liselotte and Jürgen happily accepted and laughingly agreed to celebrate "our" independence with us. Up until this point I had not paid much attention to details in the apartment. But that night I suddenly found myself in a quandary. While we were eating dinner on that warm and muggy evening, I ran around and opened all the windows in hopes of a breeze from the lake. It was then that I noticed that the windows and doors had no screens. Within fifteen minutes I ran around closing all the windows because the rooms had filled with gnats, flies, and mosquitoes. I then ran around and opened all the windows and put out all the lights in hopes that the insect kingdom would find its way out. Many eventually did, and I turned on the lights and closed the windows. It began to get warm—really warm—again.

Mopping my brow while serving dessert and trying to appear unperturbed, I asked myself if we were fated to be either overheated or in the dark. But to the others I brightly said, "You know, someone could make an absolute fortune if they introduced screens in Germany!" Liselotte and Jürgen looked quizzical. And both replied almost in unison,

"Don't they tend to keep out the fresh air?" My husband and I looked at each other, nonplussed, though sharing a quiet confidence that time would prove me right.

The second July that we spent in our apartment in Konstanz (1990), I was somewhat surprised to find no screens had yet appeared on any of the windows. Upon noting this lack, I was somehow reminded of a contrary peculiarity that really confused me: I had often observed that some of the commuters on the local un-air-conditioned buses would summarily shut a window I had just opened to relieve the heat without so much as a "do you mind?" while they muttered, "The bees and the flies will get in!"

Our good friends Liselotte and Jürgen again agreed to have dinner with us on the Fourth of July. Because the previous days had been cold and rainy and the fourth was very warm and sunny, I decided we should dine on our deck to catch the lake breeze and avoid the terrors of the dining room that I recalled. Between dusk and dark every insect in the neighborhood had collected at the four white lights illuminating the entry door to our apartment. I did find two candles which I placed on the table; and I served, ate, and scratched (I truly believe that mosquitoes prefer me to anyone else). The routine was not that different from the one I had followed the year before, except that this time I struggled with the lights on the deck and the opening and closing of the heavy glass entry door to the kitchen. My husband spent the fifth of July searching in the homeopathic pharmacies for herbal solutions that our friends had suggested to us in order to relieve the itching. I had not brought my Caladryl.

Despite these two events and some odd observations from time to time, I really liked our apartment, the city, our friends, and even the merchants at my regular shopping places, who greeted me warmly even though a year had passed. In the open market the lady-owner of the *Wurst* stand offered me tasting samples of her wares from inside the covered glass case because I pointed when I didn't know the names of all the varieties she had. She laughed quite heartily at my American accent when I attempted to pronounce the names of the few that I did know. In fact, there was one sausage to which I took a liking and bought fairly often. It came from the Polish city of Krakow (which I pronounced "Crackoff"). She always responded with, *"Ja! Ja! Sehr gut!"* in a half-mocking tone.

On this, our third-year return, when in the midst of a crowd I approached her stall, I was surprised when she greeted me with arms outstretched across the counter, almost singing, *"Willkommen, Frau Krakow!"* Surprising as that recognition was, she was yet to perplex me as well. One day while I was shopping it began to rain, and I saw my friend the *Wurst* lady, struggling with a tarpaulin in an attempt to cover her stall. I ran over to help, and at the same time inquired why she didn't look for a little shop. Would it be too expensive? "Oh, no!" she replied. "I want to be in the fresh air, not like my little sausages, always hidden behind glass."

As our final Fourth of July was approaching, we received a phone call and an invitation from our friends Liselotte and Jürgen. They said they had met a very nice couple from the University of Oregon and wanted to have us all together at their house this year. We happily accepted. They lived in Litzelstetten, a small township on soft rolling hills facing the lake just north of Konstanz. We guessed it must have been a farm that had been subdivided some time ago. The houses had been neatly placed on precise lots, though their vintages ranged from Victorian to California ranch.

Our friends' house had been built next to a very old and graceful oak tree, and under it was an elegantly set table with places for six. We arrived in a beautiful late afternoon. After introductions and drinks in the house (which, I hardly need note, was screenless), we were ushered to the table and seated. As daylight turned to dusk, Jürgen lit the candles on the table. The evening was soft and balmy, without a cloud in the sky. The conversation was lively, and the wonderful food only added to our pleasure. As darkness fell, a small cloud appeared above us. From the sound I was quick to discern that the mosquitoes were arriving. Naturally I had left my spray-can of OFF at the apartment.

Liselotte, the soul of graciousness and solicitude, appeared with a can of bug spray that she had purchased on her last trip to England —"for just such an occasion," she said. I know that she would not have used it for herself. The two Oregonians sprang to their feet in horror, declaring that using the spray would be polluting the air and damaging the universe. Seemingly abashed and responding almost too quickly, she put the can away.

Of course I began to scratch. My dear friend at once proposed that we move inside. Visions of the past danced before my eyes as I hastily and decorously declined, insisting that it would be too much trouble. Liselotte, our undaunted hostess, produced a white sheet for me. I explained to the company about my susceptibility to the small beasts in nature, and with great relief I wrapped myself from head to toe in the sheet and finished the meal seated like a ghost in the moonlight. And I wondered: after these three years, what will I be doing next year on the Fourth of July in a bug-free, screened-in, air-polluted house in Los Angeles?

Mr. Ho and the PRC

Mr. Ho and the PRC

I knew we were going to have an unusual experience when we arrived from Hong Kong at the Guangzhou (formerly Canton) airport fanning ourselves with commercially made paper fans given to us by a very cool stewardess when the air-conditioning gave out on our flight.

It was late June of 1984. My husband and I had been sent to China under the auspices of the USIS (United States Information Services), which was the name given to the USIA (United States Information Agency) in foreign countries because of earlier confusions with the CIA that had led to suspicions that the speakers they sponsored were really undercover agents sent as spies. As lecturers in the arts and literature, we found the notion laughable, but not altogether—at least not in China—as we were to find.

My husband was scheduled to lecture on American literature at the Sun Yat-sen University, and I on contemporary printmaking in the United States at the university's Art Institute. We were among the early American academic lecturers to arrive in the People's Republic after the end of the cultural revolution and the death of Mao Tse-tung.

As we disembarked from the plane, there to greet us was Mr. Ho (whose name, we discovered, was pronounced "Oh"), holding in one hand a piece of a brown paper carton with our names crudely printed on it and in the other a beautifully wrapped and ribboned spray of what I thought were a dozen lavender orchids. I later learned that the flowers were cymbidiums, a common member of the orchid family, which in my mind did not detract from their beauty, but only from their cost.

Mr. Ho was a slender young man, bespectacled and smiling, in his late twenties, I guessed. When there seemed to be a mutual look of recognition, he leaped forward and very vigorously shook hands, presented me with the flowers, and in clear English announced that he was honored to be our guide throughout our stay. He told us he had come from a poor provincial family, was almost finished as a graduate student, and was earning some extra money translating. In the same breath, while bobbing from one foot to the other, he announced that he was an avid reader and an admirer of my husband's work. I later observed that his pursed smile almost never left his face during the entire time we spent in his company during our stay, and I always hoped it was there out of joy rather than habit.

We were surprised and relieved when, by showing some sort of card, Mr. Ho whisked us out of a hot and very crowded airport and through customs in no time at all. It was still daylight and we all took a taxi, which drove us through many streets where we saw only a few small trucks. The streets were almost completely devoid of cars, although there were all manner of people on bicycles. Almost without exception, the men and women alike were wearing dark blue jackets and pants that matched. The women wore no make-up.

The impression given by the city was a somber one: many of the buildings were constructed of a dark gray cement, and the only bits of color came from the little open balconies on which laundry was strung on lines of rope, much as I remembered from the Great Depression of the thirties, when I was a child in New York City.

Our taxi came to a halt at the Great Swan Hotel, a yet-to-be-completed edifice of two thousand rooms. Until now Mr. Ho, who sat up front with the driver, had had little to say; but when we got to the hotel he whipped out his card again, showed it to the driver, then to the doorman, and again to the clerk at the desk. In a flash we had room keys in hand.

The hotel, Mr. Ho assured us, was the very best in the city, and Western style. We were not too sure what he meant by Western style, since, when we had asked about where he had learned to speak English so well, he said simply, "out of great desire," as he had never been outside of China. He further explained that China had two kinds of money, and ours was the foreigners' FEC (Foreign Exchange Currency), to be spent in hotels like this and their tourist shops; only Chinese citizens were to use their normal currency, the *Yuan*. He therefore would escort us everywhere we wished to go and indicate where we could spend our money.

The hotel, which had been two years in the building so far, was monstrously impressive. It had a huge marble lobby and a gigantic crystal chandelier almost ten feet above us and at least five feet wide. It was fully and heavily furnished, and could compare favorably with a Hilton of the 1990s.

It had been something of a struggle to get to stay in this hotel. Our hosts at the University had wanted to put us up at their guest house. However, we had been forewarned by a Chinese friend who had been there that the rooms were uncomfortable and that sanitary conditions would not be satisfactory for a spoiled Westerner. We followed his advice and insisted on a Western-style hotel, even if we had to pay for the privilege ourselves. Our hosts finally yielded, though with some resistance. The result was the Great Swan.

When looking around at the lavish lobby, I noticed that several Chinese women were sweeping the marble floors with old-fashioned, long-handled twig brooms. When I asked Mr. Ho how they cleaned the chandelier, he simply answered that the equipment for cleaning had not arrived yet. Mr. Ho saw us to our room, the style of which was much in keeping with the rest of the hotel, bid us goodnight, and said he would return to take us to our lectures that were to begin the next day.

We soon discovered that the air-conditioning in our room did not work. When I inquired at the desk, I was informed, in a very matter-of-fact way, that we had a specially assigned room (even though we were paying for it), and that a repair person would be sent as soon as possible, though probably not until the next day. Happily the room was not too uncomfortable. It overlooked an interior garden, which was all cement except for a number of small plants lining an artificial waterway, some large rocks placed helter skelter, and several very bright red-painted wooden bridges scattered here and there over the so-called running brook.

The next morning, after a breakfast that very much reflected the German nationality of the Great Swan's manager—a generous buffet of bread, cheese, cold meats, eggs, fruit, and coffee—we walked out across the street to look at a Chinese-style hotel. It was bustling with humanity, quite dog-eared, but it did indeed have a carefully maintained and blooming mature garden in front, though only the ghost of a babbling brook remained.

Within seconds of our appointed time Mr. Ho arrived, and he seemed unhappy when we mentioned the garden across the street, because we had not waited for him to take us there. But he then added that he would make up for it at the university. He informed us that Guangzhou had been a great garden city and that the university used to have the most spectacular flowers in southern China. During the cultural revolution, however, gardening had to be replaced by farming, so that sweet potatoes and peanuts were cultivated instead of flowers. Now, as restrictions were easing, the return to gardening was beginning to show. The university gardens, however, still showed many signs of needing repair.

By the time my husband and I finished our first series of lectures at the university, with Mr. Ho serving as introducer, translator, clarifier, and receiver of questions addressed to the podium from the university president on down to the students, we began to feel a bit ill at ease. Mr. Ho was stuck to us like glue. And when we recalled that he had requested permission for all the lectures to be taped—in order, he said, to be distributed to other universities throughout China—and, further, that he regretted there would not be time for my husband to hear them before they were sent to Beijing, I could see in my husband's eyes as they met mine, "Censorship!" "But of what?" I asked myself, thinking of the political innocence of our subjects.

As we were walking toward the statue of Sun Yat-sen at the center of the schoolgrounds, we came upon a lovely looking young woman and a small child. Mr. Ho jumped forward and said he would like to introduce us to his wife, Mei-ling, and son, whose name I could not make out. He added that they did not speak English yet but would be learning soon. She shook our hands shyly, but with a very warm and responsive smile. But when I extended my hand to his son, the boy recoiled, his face darkening as he grabbed his mother's jacket and jumped behind her. Mr. Ho interceded and again, in a very straightforward manner, asked me not to be disturbed. It had not occurred to him that in the children's books that were read to his son, the she-devil was always described and pictured with white hair (mine was blonde) and a painted face (my lipstick was very red, and my blue eyes did not help the situation). He assured me that this misreading would all be very easily straightened out once he explained it to his son.

Back at our hotel, while walking back and forth in the corridor outside our room, we decided that any real conversation we might have should be carried on out there, as we felt sure that our room was bugged. And inside the room, one or the other of us, almost in a routine way, would point knowingly at the ceiling light fixture in order to restrict our conversation to meaningless pleasantries, in a manner consistent with our recollections of Hollywood's 007. In the halls we talked freely of our impressions and worried about Mr. Ho's real role as our inescapable and jolly companion.

Our meals outside the hotel were spectacular. Mr. Ho strongly urged that we never refuse a "banquet," mainly for the sake of the faculty visiting from the provinces and the graduate students. He explained that a banquet meant that for the honored guests there would be anywhere from twenty-four to twenty-nine dishes, magnificently prepared and served; and they certainly were! This would be especially appreciated by Chinese colleagues, whose diet was usually quite minimal. Such a variety of food was simply not available, and if it had been, the cost would have been prohibitive.

On one of our corridor strolls, my husband and I went 'round and 'round about Mr. Ho. We decided that, despite his nervous demeanor, he was wholly in control; that he had a very wry humor, was very intelligent, and surely was very helpful and solicitous to us, so that despite his persistent and never-ending picture-taking and his never allowing us a moment's peace without bombarding us with questions about our professions, home, children, travels, philosophy and literature, we could not help liking him. Amazingly, politics had never come up in our conversations with him. Still, we could not altogether eliminate our wariness. Indeed, after having met many Chinese academics who had studied English extensively and yet spoke it poorly, there seemed no way to account for Mr. Ho's excellent English except to suspect that he was trained in a government school for special agents. All these strands spun a complicated web.

By the time of our last evening in Guangzhou, we assumed that we had passed all the tests when Mr. Ho asked us for two favors before he took us to the airport: first, that we permit him to shower in our bathroom and, second, that he take us to his student apartment for tea—"old persons' tea," a rather formal ritual where tea is drunk from miniature cups, and toasts and farewells are given. In fact, tea was the formal and informal farewell to everything. Mr. Ho carried a pot, two old cups, and a small cloth to every lecture, and after the last question of every session he poured and sipped with my husband or me at the podium.

Of course, we happily agreed to Mr. Ho's requests and at once brought him to our room to shower. Because we had been concerned during our visit to the faculty and student quarters by their spare and neglected condition, my husband and I began to fill a plastic laundry bag with the hotel's complimentary provisions for its guests—soap, kleenex, toilet paper, pencils and writing paper. Mr. Ho went along with the idea once we insisted that he distribute these at school. We told him that we had been upset to find that, other than the employees, there was not another Chinese person in the hotel, except for a small number of dignitaries, who we had noticed were being escorted in a group. All of us in collusion went on to place in the bag even the small bottles of whiskey and anything else we could pay for from the bar. We departed from the hotel feeling rather self-satisfied, and, after tea in his meager apartment, departed from China promising to stay in correspondence with Mr. Ho.

Six years later, in August 1990, as we were preparing for another lecture tour in the far east, this time mainly in India by way of Hong Kong, we decided to stop over briefly in Guangzhou in response to Mr. Ho, who had written us pleadingly, asking us to see him at least for a dinner. Were we going because of affection for him, or because of a lingering political curiosity?

There again at the airport was Mr. Ho, with flowers in hand. With him were Mei-ling (whom we now were to call Lena), and their son (now to be called Danny). They ran up to greet us with hugs. This time Lena wore a skirt and blouse, and Danny wore the UCLA tee-shirt we had sent him some time ago. Mr. Ho, with his very recognizable smile, responded to our greeting by saying, "As you know, my given name is Te-hsing, but would you favor me from now on by calling me by the English name I have taken—Max?" Max it was from then on.

They at once took us to their very modest faculty apartment, which was made available to him now that he was teaching at the university. Lena prepared a wonderful meal, which Danny served while we all spoke in various levels of English. On the wall was a collection of photos, some of which included us on our visit five years before. But I was more surprised when I saw the inexpensive and very typical silver-and-turquoise American Indian necklace that I had brought for Lena when we last visited. It was beautifully framed and hung on the wall as if it were a work of art. When I inquired about it, Lena replied that, though she loved it, women did not wear jewelry then, so she felt the proper place to display it was at home.

At dinner there was a more shocking surprise. Max told us he had been invited for a second time to teach as a visitor in the United States. He desperately wanted to come in order to complete some research on a book he was writing. But because he had expressed some anti-government views and had gone to Beijing to participate in the Tiananmen Square demonstrations, he was concerned about getting permission to leave. The year before, when he received his first invitation, he was sure that his papers had been held up so that he could not accept. But he still hoped for better luck this time.

I was inwardly abashed at our earlier paranoia and the lingering suspicions it fostered. We departed after having "old persons' tea" served from the new set we brought with us as a gift for Max and Lena from Hong Kong.

Tomorrow we look forward to greeting Max at the Los Angeles airport. Lena and Danny were not given permission to leave China, perhaps to ensure Max's return. So he comes alone, and with his own confused (or is it *our* confused?) notions about his country and ours. And I cannot help wondering how the ways of this land will strike Max (or is he still really Mr. Ho?)—ways at once foreign and familiar.

The computer graphics in this book were produced on a Macintosh SE/30 and Macintosh Laserwriter II, using Superpaint 2.0 and Mac Calligraphy 2.0; and on a PC 386 and HP Laserjet II, using Pagemaker 4.0.